DISCARD

THE PILLOW WAR

THE PiLLOW WAR

Matt Novak

ORCHARD BOOKS   NEW YORK

Orchard Books, 95 Madison Avenue, New York, NY 10016

Manufactured in the United States of America   Printed by Barton Press, Inc.
Bound by Horowitz/Rae   Book design by Mina Greenstein

The text of this book is set in 22 point Weiss Bold.
The illustrations are acrylic paintings in full color.
10   9   8   7   6   5   4   3   2   1

Library of Congress Cataloging-in-Publication Data
Novak, Matt. The Pillow War / by Matt Novak.   p.   cm.
Summary: When a brother and sister have a pillow fight to decide which of them
will get to sleep with the dog, their battle escalates to engulf the world.
ISBN 0-531-30048-X. — ISBN 0-531-33048-6 (lib. bdg.)
[1. Brothers and sisters—Fiction.   2. Fighting (Psychology)—Fiction.
3. Stories in rhyme.]   I. Title.   PZ8.3.N8555Pi   1997
[E]—dc21   96-53864

For my sister, Mary

The Pillow War started when Millie and Fred
went up to their room to get ready for bed.

Millie and Fred had a little dog, Sam.
"I'm his best friend," said Millie. Fred said, "I am."

Millie called to the dog, "Sleep with me. Warm my toes."
Fred called even louder, "Sam, come here. Lick my nose."
"He's my dog!" yelled Millie, and Fred yelled, "He's mine!"
Then Millie bopped Fred. It was pillow fight time.

They fought down the stairs

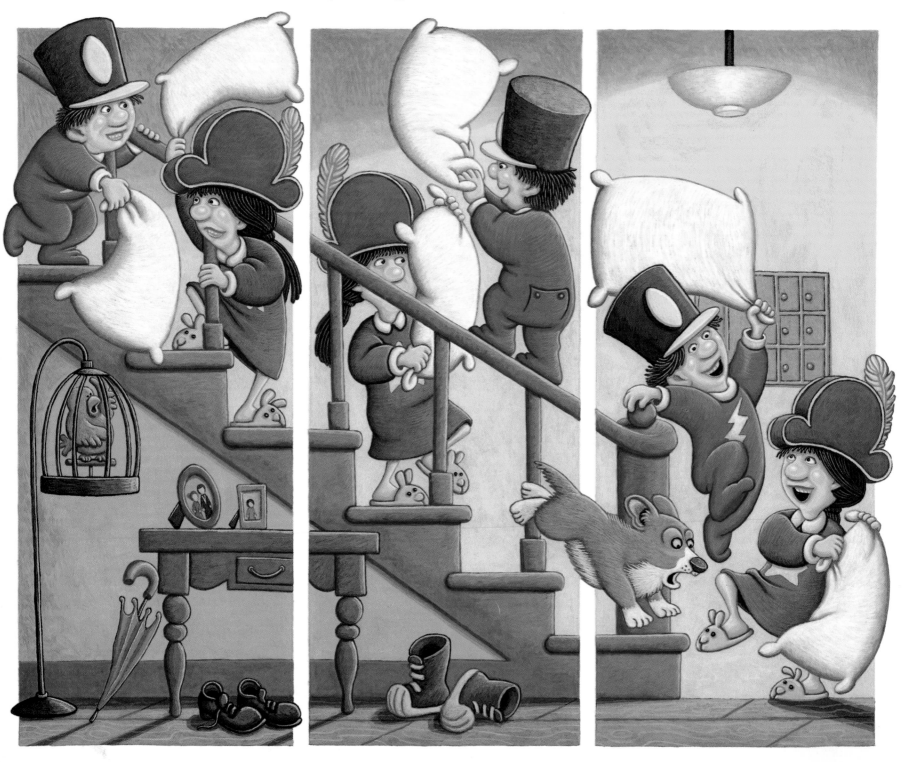

out into the street,

where their neighbors joined in

with pillows and sheets.

They fought on the land

as the battle grew.

They fought on the seas,

and the feathers flew.

Into the air

they whirled and twirled

until the war raged all over the world.

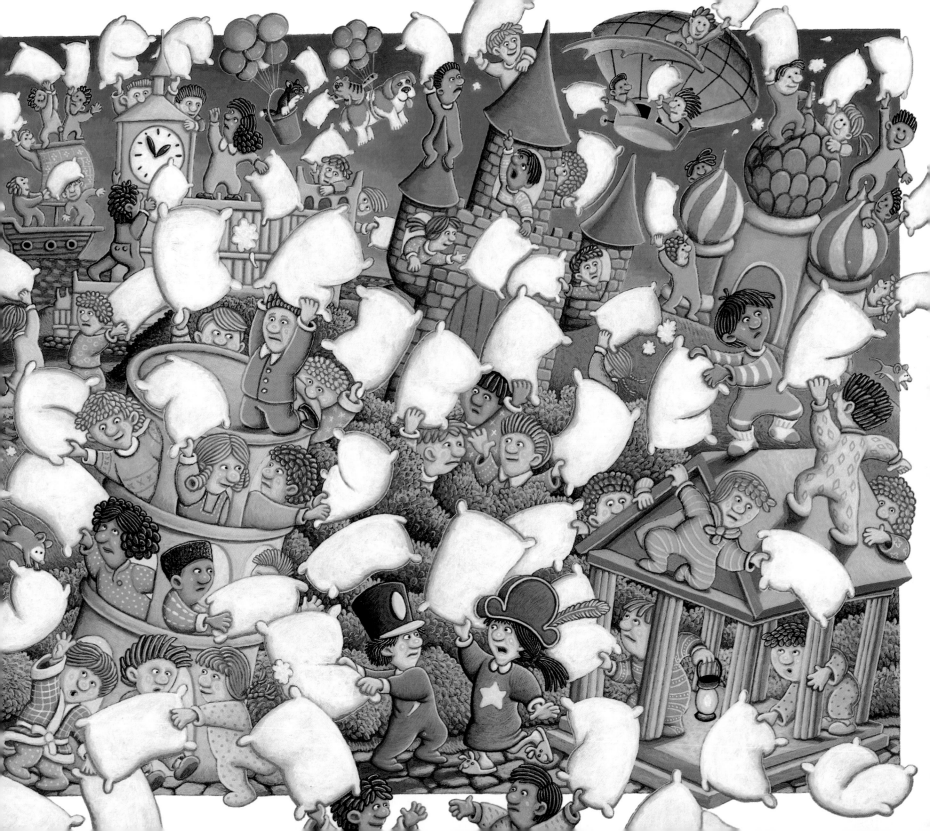

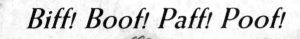

Then Fred got hurt, and Millie yelled, "Halt!"

"The war is over. It was all my fault."

She carried Fred home, and she put him to bed.

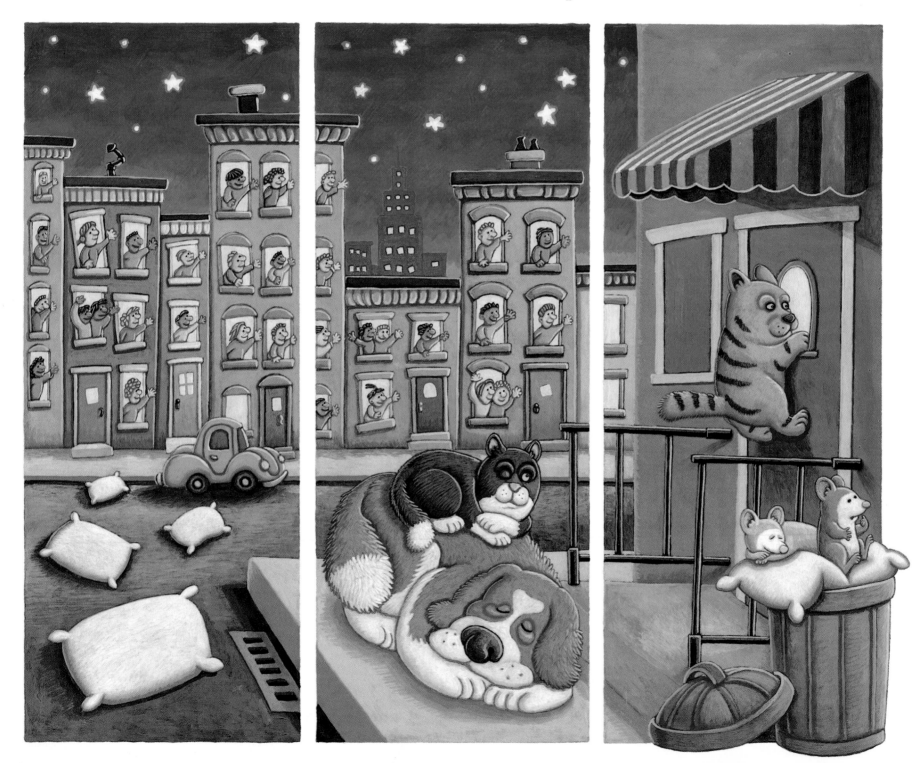

"I'm sorry," she cried. "Me too," said Fred.

"We'll take turns," Millie said. "We don't need to fight.
I'll take Sam tomorrow. You take him tonight."

They called upstairs and downstairs, all over their home.
But Sam did not answer. . . .

He liked sleeping alone.